ANIMALS
ON
THE EDGE
HIPPO

ANIMALS
ON
THE EDGE
HIPPO

by Anna Claybourne

BLOOMSBURY

LONDON BERLIN NEW YORK SYDNEY

Published 2012 by
Bloomsbury Publishing Plc
50 Bedford Square, London, WC1B 3DP

www.bloomsbury.com

ISBN HB 978-1-4081-4826-6
ISBN PB 978-1-4081-4961-4

Picture acknowledgements:
Cover: Shutterstock
Insides: All Shutterstock except for the following; p8 ©Jon Bodsworth via Wikimedia
Commons, p13 ©ZSL, p14 top ©ZSL, p15 top ©ZSL, p15 bottom ©F. York/ZSL, p18
©ZSL, p19 all images ©ZSL, p21 bottom ©ZSL, p22 ©ZSL, p 23 all images ©ZSL, p 26
bottom © KS_aus_F via Wikimedia Commons, p27 bottom ©Robert D. Ward via Wikimedia
Commons, p28 ©ZSL, p29 top ©USAID [CC-BY-SA-3.0] via Wikimedia Commons, p30
bottom left ©Ben Collen/ZSL, p31 top ©John Etherton/johnetherton.com, p32 top ©Robert
How/FFI, p32 bottom ©Ben Collen/ZSL, p33 top ©John Etherton/johnetherton.com,
p34 ©ZSL, p35 all images ©ZSL, p36 © Michael Lyster/ZSL, p37 bottom ©Tim Ross via
Wikimedia Commons, p40 ©Gil Hidalgo (Central Florida Zoo), via Wikimedia Commons

Manufactured and supplied under licence from the Zoological Society of London.

Produced for Bloomsbury Publishing Plc by Geoff Ward.

A CIP catalogue for this book is available from the British Library.

Printed in China by C&C Offset Printing Co.

MIX
Paper from
responsible sources
FSC
www.fsc.org   FSC® C008047

CONTENTS

MEET THE HIPPOPOTAMUS

A hippopotamus looks bulky and round – even cuddly. You might think it's a calm, slow animal. But hippos are surprising! They are strong, can run faster than us, and make a bellowing sound as loud as thunder. When a hippo opens its huge jaws, it reveals long, sharp teeth. If you ever do meet a hippopotamus, don't get too close!

Where in the world?

In the wild, hippos live in Africa. You could meet them on land, or in a river or lake. They feed on grass and other land plants, but spend most of the day in the water, resting and sheltering from the sun.

Two hippos

There are two types, or **species**, of hippos. They look similar in shape and colour – but there's one BIG difference! The common hippo can grow to 5m long, and weigh 3,000kg – as much as 35 people. It's one of the biggest land animals on Earth. The pygmy hippo is *much* smaller – up to 175cm long and weighing 270kg, the same as about three people. That's still a large animal, though – you wouldn't want it to tread on your toe!

A common hippo has a big, bulky, square-ish body, and its ears and eyes are on top of its head.

Endangered species

A worldwide organisation called the International Union for Conservation of Nature decides which animals are most at risk of dying out, and keeps lists of them. The common hippo is listed as a **vulnerable** species, meaning it is not **endangered**, but could be soon. But the pygmy hippo is already an endangered species. This means it is in danger of dying out, and becoming extinct. In this book, you can find out about hippo **conservation** – how we are helping common hippos, and trying to save pygmy hippos from disappearing.

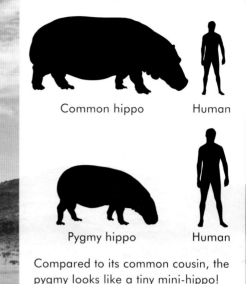

Common hippo   Human

Pygmy hippo   Human

Compared to its common cousin, the pygmy looks like a tiny mini-hippo!

The smaller pygmy hippo's body is more smooth and rounded. Its ears and eyes are on the sides of its head.

WHAT DO YOU CALL LOTS OF HIPPOS?

Apart from "hippos", the plural of hippopotamus is usually "hippopotamuses". There's also a more old-fashioned plural, "hippopotami". A group of hippopotamuses is known as a herd, a **pod** or a **bloat**!

Do you get hippos mixed up with rhinos? It's easy to tell them apart – rhinos have horns on their noses, and hippos haven't.

FACT FILE: LATIN NAMES

Scientists give each living thing its own scientific name, written in Latin.

Common hippo   *Hippopotamus amphibius*
Meaning: "River horse of land and water"

Pygmy hippo   *Choeropsis liberiensis*
Meaning: "Pig-like animal of Liberia"

TALES OF THE HIPPO

The hippopotamus has fascinated humans for thousands of years. Throughout history, there have been all sorts of bizarre beliefs and stories about hippos. Some are magical, but made-up... and some are strange but true!

Hippo helper

The ancient Egyptians had a hippo goddess, Taweret. She was said to help mothers and guard their babies, as people saw how fiercely mother hippos defended their young.

Egyptian goddess Tarewet had the head of a hippo.

Horse of the water

The ancient Greeks thought that hippos were like horses. Greek writer Herodotus said: "This animal has four legs, cloven hoofs like cattle, a blunt nose, a horse's mane and tail, visible tusks, and neighs like a horse." As you can tell, Herodotus had never even seen a hippo! His description probably came from garbled travellers' tales.

Sweating blood?

When early explorers saw thick, reddish slimy stuff on hippos, they thought they were sweating blood. In fact, this is not sweat or blood – although it is called **"blood sweat"**. It's an oily red liquid that hippos make in their skin to protect them from sunburn. It also kills germs.

A light in the night

In Liberia, where pygmy hippos live, there are many folk tales about them. One says that each hippo carries a shining diamond in its mouth to light its way along the forest paths at night. During the day, it hides its diamond somewhere safe.

A bird on the back

In cartoons you'll often see a hippo with a small bird sitting on its back. This really does happen. The bird, called an oxpecker, nibbles lice, fleas and other pests from the skin of larger animals like hippos. The hippo gets cleaned, while the bird gets a snack!

This lucky hippo has two oxpecker birds searching for snacks on its head.

The hippo's oily skin-protector can make it look pinkish-red.

Owen and Mzee

In 2004, when a huge **tsunami** struck the Indian Ocean, a baby hippo became separated from his mother. Wildlife rangers took him to a **wildlife reserve** to recover. There, the hippo, named Owen, met Mzee, a 100-year-old giant tortoise. Mzee looked after Owen and let him snuggle up to him. They became best friends, and stayed together for over two years, until Owen was placed with a female hippo.

Surfing hippo

Hippos usually prefer fresh water in rivers, lakes or swamps. But once in a while, a hippo wanders out into the sea. They have been spotted bobbing up and down in the waves and searching for food on the beach.

HIPPOS IN THE WILD

Hippos LOVE water, and are always found around rivers or lakes. Water is the hippo's sanctuary, where it feels safe. Hippos usually only leave the water or pool to eat grass and other plants, mostly in the evening or at night.

Under the water

Hippos can't breathe underwater. But they can hold their breath for several minutes at a time, and close their ears and nostrils tightly to keep the water out. In the water, a hippo's heavy weight is supported, and it can prance and leap like a ballet dancer along the river bottom.

Hippo herds

Common hippos live in groups, or pods, of around 20 hippos. There is usually one chief male or **bull**, a herd of females and their babies, and some other male hippos who hang out together. Pygmy hippos are more solitary. They usually live alone or in twos – either a male and a female, or a mother with her baby.

A common hippo takes a dive, with its ears and nostrils sealed.

"Hey – I live here!"

Common hippos – the bigger variety – have a **territory**, an area of the river they consider their own. They guard it fiercely. Male hippos fight violent battles with each other over territory. Pygmy hippos don't care so much about territory, but they do like to avoid other hippos.

A hippo can mark its territory in a very smelly way! As it does a poo, its spins its tail around, flinging and spreading the poo over a wide area. Pygmy hippos do this too, to show other hippos where they have been. This helps them to stay out of each other's way.

When they have a fight, hippos show just how scary and violent they can be.

Like hippos, whales are **mammals** that hold their breath underwater.

THE HIPPO AND THE WHALE

Hippos' closest relatives are not horses, as the ancient Greeks thought, and not elephants or rhinos, although they look a bit like them. In fact, scientists have found that the animals that are most similar to hippos are whales!

To steer a little boat like this on an African river, you have to be very careful and watch out for hippos at all times.

DEADLY HIPPOS

Common hippos are incredibly dangerous – they kill hundreds of people each year. They can charge and trample anyone who gets in between them and their favourite patch of water, or comes near their young. They also overturn boats that bother them, and can even bite a small boat in two!

THE PYGMY HIPPO

Pygmy hippos are rare, shy, and hard to find. Unlike their bigger cousins, common hippos, they are rarely aggressive. They would usually rather hide than attack. In fact, they are so secretive, people rarely see them in the wild. Even experts, who know exactly what to look for, have trouble tracking them down.

Life in the forest

While common hippos prefer grasslands, pygmy hippos live mainly in forests and swamps. They are found in just four small African countries: Liberia, Sierra Leone, Côte d'Ivoire, and Guinea. During the day, they wallow in rivers, streams, muddy hollows or swamps. In the evening, they follow trails through the thick forests to feed on grass, leaves and fruit.

Lush, swampy African forests like this are the home of the pygmy hippo.

AFRICA

Common

Pygmy

DID YOU KNOW?

Scientists from outside Africa weren't even sure the pygmy hippo existed until around 100 years ago.

Hippos in danger

Like many wild animals, hippos are in trouble – *especially* the pygmy hippo, which is endangered. Numbers of both types of hippos are falling. Common hippos, which are classed as a vulnerable species, live in many parts of Africa, and there are around 125,000 of them in the wild. But pygmy hippos are only found in a small part of West Africa. No one knows exactly how many are left. It's probably around 2,000 to 3,000 but could be less.

On the Edge

The pygmy hippo is an **EDGE** focal species. **ZSL**, the Zoological Society of London, runs the EDGE of Existence conservation programme for animals that are rare, unusual, and have few relatives. If they die out, there will be nothing like them left in the world. The pygmy hippo is a typical example. It has only one close relative, the common hippo. It's extremely rare, only found in one area, and at risk of extinction.

PYGMY PARTS

The pygmy hippo is specially **adapted**, or suited, to life in its forest **habitat**. It has some features that make it different from common hippos, as you can see here:

Skin is dark blackish-green on top, and paler below.

Rounded snout that helps the hippo push its way through forest plants.

Separate toes with sharp claws, for running through the undergrowth, (common hippos have webbed toes).

Eyes are on the sides of the head, not the front as in the common hippo. This may help the pygmy hippo look out for danger.

HIPPOS IN ZOOS

Both common hippos and pygmy hippos live in zoos. You can go and visit them there, get a good, close look at them – and hear and smell them too!

What a hippo needs

In its enclosure, a hippo needs plenty of outdoor space to wander around, explore and get some exercise. There should also be muddy patches to roll in, and trees and bushes for shade. Hippos also have an indoor area where they can shelter from the weather, hide from visitors if they are feeling shy, or even take a shower!

Of course, all hippos also need water. Their enclosure must have a nice big pool, pond or canal for bathing, wallowing and relaxing in. It has to be deep enough to let the hippos dive right under the water.

Lola, one of ZSL Whipsnade's common hippos, heads into the hippo pool for a relaxing wallow.

In some zoos, the hippos' pools are filled with cichlids, a type of African freshwater fish. They feed on hippo poo!

Happy hippos

Pygmy hippos mainly live alone in the wild, and some have their own zoo enclosures too. Others live happily together in a male and female couple. Common hippos are more sociable, and like to spend time together, so they can be kept in larger groups.

Because they're smaller, pygmy hippos get cold more easily, and like to shelter or sleep indoors in chilly weather. Big common hippos are a bit tougher and don't mind winter weather so much.

Safe in the zoo

Keeping hippos in zoos is one way to help them survive as a species. It keeps their numbers up, especially if they can **breed** and have babies. It also makes it easier for scientists to study them closely, and learn more about them and how to help them.

Some seriously endangered species, such as the scimitar-horned oryx, have died out in the wild, and only survive in zoos and wildlife parks. It's possible that this could happen to the pygmy hippo, if we don't work hard to help it now.

The outdoor part of the pygmy hippo enclosure at ZSL London Zoo.

THE FAMOUS OBAYSCH

The first ever common hippo at ZSL London Zoo arrived in the year 1850. His name was Obaysch and he was captured from the wild as a baby, in the River Nile. The Victorians flocked to see him, even though he was famous for his grumpiness.

This old photo shows Obaysch enjoying a lie down in his enclosure, with his female mate Adhela.

FEEDING TIME

All hippos are vegetarians, and only eat plant food. Plants aren't as full of energy as meat, so plant-eaters have to eat a lot to keep them going. And because hippos are so big, they are extra-hungry!

In the grasslands

Common hippos leave the water at dusk and walk to their feeding grounds, where there's plenty of grass and other plants. A hippo can walk 5-10km on a feeding trip, **graze** for five hours, and eat as much as 60 kilos of food.

This common hippo calf is nibbling at plants on the riverbank.

In the forest

Pygmy hippos set off to feed in the evening, munch their way along the forest trails, and return at around midnight. In the forests and swamps where they live, there isn't much grass. Instead, they eat ferns, leaves, roots, young plant **shoots**, fruit that's fallen to the ground, and sometimes water plants. As they are smaller, they eat less food – around five kilos per night.

Hippo wind!

Inside a hippo, food moves through the stomach, which has three sections, and into the **intestines**. Tiny **bacteria** help to break down the grass and other plant food. This creates quite a lot of smelly gas. It comes out of both the front and back ends of the hippo!

In the zoo

Hippos in zoos are usually fed a mixture of clover or hay (dried grass), tree branches, fruit and vegetables such as melons, beetroots and lettuce, and special "herbivore pellets". They contain cereal, oil and vitamins.

HIPPO FOOD SHOPPING LIST

Here's a typical shopping list for zoo hippos' meals:

For the pygmy hippos:

Clover
Lettuce
Cabbage
Alfalfa
Sweet potatoes
Carrots
Apples
Celery
Bread rolls
Tree branches
Herbivore pellets

For the common hippos:

Hay
Lettuce
Alfalfa
Melons
Beetroot
Herbivore pellets

Zoo hippos tucking into a variety of different foods: grass, fruit, vegetables and sliced bread!

HIPPO POO

Just like cows, horses and other plant-munchers, hippos produce a lot of poo. They usually poo in the water, and it sinks to the bottom. Keepers have to clean it up using a suction hose, a bit like an underwater vacuum cleaner.

A DAY IN THE LIFE: PYGMY HIPPO KEEPER

Tracey Lee works at London Zoo as a Head Keeper, and has a lot of experience looking after its pair of pygmy hippos, Thug and Nicola (known as Nicky-Noo!). She explains what a hippo keeper does all day, and what it's like getting close to a real hippo!

A zookeeper's day

7:30am First thing in the morning, Nicky and Thug are fed. In the wild, pygmy hippos like eating plants that grow in rivers, so one thing they love is clover soaked in a bucket of water. Thug has an overgrown tusk, so the keepers have trained him to open his mouth and let them file it down, in return for a handful of tasty herbivore pellets.

9.00am It's time for the hippos to go outside, while the keepers clean their inside dens. Pygmy hippos like to spray their poo everywhere with their tails, so lots of elbow grease is needed to keep their enclosures clean. It's a bit of a smelly job!

This is Tracey Lee, a keeper who works at ZSL London Zoo with pygmy hippos Thug and Nicky.

COMMON HIPPO CARE

Common hippos are much bigger than pymgy hippos, and more dangerous. They need extra-strong fencing, and the keepers have to be careful not to get in their way. They like to spend most of the day wallowing in water, so they need bigger pools than pygmy hippos too.

10.00am From now on, the hippos will spend most of the day in their paddock, or outdoor area. Thug likes to hang out submerged in the pool like a mini submarine, whereas Nicky likes to sleep in the shelter. We scatter clover and browse (tree branches to nibble) around the enclosure for them.

4.00pm At night, we call the hippos into their indoor dens, where they have a dinner of clover and browse. They'll sleep for much of the night, on beds made of soft, fine soil that's gentle on their delicate skin.

Keeper Tracey is feeding Thug and Nicky some delicious leaves in their indoor enclosure.

ALL CHANGE!

Twice a year, as the seasons change, the pygmy hippos move from their winter enclosure to their summer enclosure, and vice-versa. This is one of the most exciting moments of the year, as they have to walk across the public path. Photographers from the newspapers often come to catch their journey on camera.

ZSL London Zoo keeper Paul Kybett is training Thug to open his mouth so they can file down his teeth.

HAVING BABIES

Like humans, all hippos are mammals. They don't lay eggs; instead, they give birth to live babies. Mother hippos make milk in their bodies for their babies to feed on, and care for them as they grow up.

Meeting a mate

In the wild, common hippo herds have a bull hippo, a big, **dominant** male. He fights other males for the position of leader, and he is the only one that mates with the female hippos. He is the father of all the babies that are born in the herd. As pygmy hippos don't live in herds, a male and a female have to find each other in order to mate.

GROWING UP

Weight at birth: Common hippo 30-40 kilos; Pygmy hippo 4-6 kilos

0-3 weeks: Only feeds on mother's milk.

3 weeks: Begins eating grass or other plants.

6-8 months: Stops feeding on milk.

3-6 years: Young hippos become adults and can have their own babies.

Hippo lifespan: Common hippo about 50 years; Pygmy hippo about 40 years.

This baby hippo gets tired easily, so its mother gives it a helping hand by letting it ride on her back.

A mother common hippo stays close to her calf as it explores the river shallows.

Baby hippos

A common hippo calf grows inside its mother for 8 months, and weighs 30-40 kilos at birth – as much as a large dog. Baby pygmy hippos are much smaller, weighing around 4-6 kilos – only slightly bigger than a human baby.

Hippos usually have their babies in the water, although they can give birth on land. Usually, a mother has one calf at a time, but hippos do sometimes have twins. Once the baby is born, it stays close to its mum, feeding on her milk, and nuzzling up to her.

HIPPO MYSTERIES

Scientists have recently learned a lot about pygmy hippos in the wild. But they still haven't learned everything about how they breed outside of zoos, as pygmy hippos are so hard to find.

This is Sapo, a baby pygmy hippo born in 2011 at ZSL Whipsnade Zoo.

Zoo babies

Some animals in zoos have problems having babies – but hippos seem to be good at it. Both common and pygmy hippos have calves quite often, in zoos around the world. It's always exciting for zookeepers and the public when a baby is born.

HIPPO FAMILY: FLORA, TAPON AND SAPO

Pygmy hippos Flora and Tapon live at ZSL Whipsnade Zoo in Dunstable, Bedfordshire. They are a couple, and are the parents of baby Sapo, born in 2011.

What are they like?

Tapon is 20 years younger than Flora, but they have been a happy couple since they first met. Flora is quite laid-back, whereas Tapon can be a bit grumpy, but he still likes a scratch and stroke from his keepers.

Apart and together

Tapon and Flora live separately, but once in a while, they show signs of being ready to mate. These signs include making a mess of the areas where they sleep, and making grunting or honking noises. Flora will also put her front feet on the side of the walls of her enclosure to try and get a glimpse of Tapon.

Flora lovingly nuzzles baby Sapo as he explores the pool.

When this happens, the keepers put the two pygmy hippos together in one enclosure for a few days. They are separated at night, so they can sleep easily. During that time, they may mate. This is what happened in 2010, when Flora became pregnant with their first baby.

Hello Sapo!

Pygmy hippo calf Sapo was born in March 2011. He was named after a national park in Liberia where pygmy hippos live in the wild (see page 32). Sapo loves to play hide and seek, and sometimes the keepers can't find him as he likes to bury himself deep in his hay bed. He sleeps on hay rather than soil, as he eats everything he sees and the keepers are worried he will gobble up his bedding! Sapo fed on his mother's milk for his first six months or so, but started eating his greens as well from the age of three months.

Daddy Tapon lives separately from Sapo and his mum, the same as happens in the wild.

Sapo has a good nose at a TV camera on his first day of being on show to the public.

GOING ON SHOW

When he was first born, Sapo was kept away from visitors so that he and his mum Flora could get to know each other in peace and quiet. But when he was three months old, he was revealed to the public for the first time. News reporters and photographers came too, to see Sapo take his first dip in the outdoor pool.

THREATS TO HIPPOS

Why are hippos, especially pygmy hippos, so at risk?
When animals become endangered, there are
usually lots of reasons, not just one.

Space to live in

The biggest problem for pygmy hippos in particular, like many other endangered species, is **habitat loss**. Habitat means the surroundings that a species is suited to living in. For a pygmy hippo, that means the swampy, damp jungles of West Africa, and the rivers and streams that run through them.

Habitat loss usually happens because humans take over areas that used to be wild. The number of people keeps going up and up, and we take up more and more space. In West Africa, the wild forests are being **logged** (cut down) for their timber, and to make space for mining, farming, roads and homes.

All that's left of what was once a forest, after its trees have been cut down.

Habitat in bits

Even if some wild habitat is left, it's often split up into smaller sections, separated by farms and villages, or criss-crossed by roads. This is called **habitat fragmentation**. It makes it hard for pygmy hippos to move around to find food, and to find each other so that they can have babies.

Bushmeat

Although hunting pygmy hippos is not allowed, **poaching** (illegal hunting) still happens. People hunt the hippos for **bushmeat** – meat that comes from wild animals. A pygmy hippo, of course, is easier to catch and kill than a much bigger common hippo, but it still provides a lot of meat.

WHY DO PEOPLE HUNT THE HIPPO?

It's sad to think of people killing and eating an endangered pygmy hippo, but they may have good reasons. In some parts of Africa, many people are very poor, and there are sometimes famines when they actually begin to starve. If you were in that situation, you might hunt wild animals for food too.

This common hippo calf has sadly died, perhaps because of losing its mother to hunters.

At markets in Africa you can often find bushmeat from many different wild animals species for sale.

COMMON HIPPO THREATS

Common hippos are also at risk from hunting, though not always for the same reasons. In the past, hunters went to Africa to kill the biggest, most dangerous animals they could find, just for fun. Many hippos died this way. Today, hunters kill common hippos for meat, and also to use their large teeth as a kind of ivory (which also comes from elephants' tusks).

HIPPOS IN WARS

Hippos don't fight in wars, but wars are bad news for them, especially the endangered pygmy hippo. Liberia and Sierra Leone, two of the countries where pygmy hippos live, have suffered terrible civil wars, with different armies fighting each other for power. But how can wars harm hippos?

No rules

During a civil war, there is no fixed government. The **government** of a country makes the laws, and runs a police force to catch anyone who breaks them. But without a proper government, this can't happen, so it's much easier to break the law. That means people can hunt more hippos, or chop down forests that are supposed to be protected.

BLOOD DIAMONDS

Liberia and Sierra Leone both have a lot of underground diamonds. During the civil wars, some armies began mining and selling diamonds to make more money for fighting. They were known as blood diamonds. Unfortunately, mining, especially if it's not controlled by strict laws, can also damage the pygmy hippo's habitat.

Civil war fighters usually have guns, so it's easy for them to kill wild animals for food, or to make extra money for their armies.

No money

Governments also pay for some conservation schemes to help wildlife. But in a civil war, wildlife is often forgotten. Everyone is more worried about winning the war, and all the money gets spent on weapons.

No workers

Conservation needs people, too – to guard endangered species, study them, and run **national parks** where they can live in safety. During wars, conservation workers may join the fighting, escape to safety in another country, or even die in battles. Experts from other countries can't enter the country to help the animals either, as it's too dangerous.

This tank has been left abandoned after a war, damaging the countryside.

In West Africa, a lot of small countries are packed tightly together.

WHAT WARS, AND WHY?

West Africa's civil wars mainly happened when **rebel** armies tried to overthrow leaders. In Liberia, there were two wars, from 1989-1996, and 1999-2003. One Liberian leader, Charles Taylor, helped rebel armies to fight their own war in Sierra Leone, from 1991-2002. These wars killed around 400,000 people. After they ended, both countries became more stable, and held **elections** to find new leaders. Conservation work began again, bringing new hope for pygmy hippos.

In 2005, Liberia elected a new president, Ellen Johnson Sirleaf, who has shown her support for pygmy hippo conservation.

IS THERE ANYBODY OUT THERE...?

In 2008, workers from the EDGE of Existence programme set out to look for pygmy hippos in Sapo National Park in Liberia. After the civil wars that had ravaged the country, no one was sure if these endangered hippos had survived...

Spotted!

As pygmy hippos are so shy and hard to spot, camera traps were used to try to find them. To the workers' delight, the camera traps did reveal that pygmy hippos were alive and well, and exploring Sapo's forests by night. They also showed lots of other interesting animal species. Now it was time to work on a plan to help them.

Help for hippos

In 2010 the Zoological Society of London helped to set up the most important pygmy hippo meeting to date. All four countries where the hippo lives – Liberia, Sierra Leone, Guinea and Côte d'Ivoire – got together with experts from ZSL, the IUCN, which lists threatened species, and other animal conservation experts.

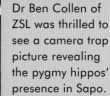

Dr Ben Collen of ZSL was thrilled to see a camera trap picture revealing the pygmy hippos' presence in Sapo.

Sapo contains a large area of "primary" rainforest - forest that has never been cut down or changed by humans.

Common hippos are sometimes hunted by poachers who use their teeth as a kind of ivory (which also comes from elephants).

COMMON HIPPO

The common hippo is vulnerable, rather than endangered, but there are conservation projects to help it too. ZSL has campaigned to protect hippos at Virunga National Park in the Congo, where they are in danger from poachers.

Making a plan

At the 2010 meeting, everyone agreed a plan, or Species Conservation Strategy, for pygmy hippos. It set up a list of things to do, including:

- More monitoring and studying, to find out as much as possible about existing pygmy hippos.
- Checking for hippos in other areas besides Sapo, such as the Loma Mountains in Sierra Leone.

- Asking each of the four governments to highlight the pygmy hippo as an especially important "flagship" species, to make their people more aware of it and proud of it.
- Asking the governments to improve laws against hippo poaching.
- Focusing on the areas where pygmy hippos live, to protect them from poaching, mining, building, logging and other problems.

A DAY IN THE LIFE: PYGMY HIPPO SURVEYOR

Dr Ben Collen is a scientist. He has been to Sapo National Park to set up camera traps to monitor pygmy hippos. He describes what's it like to trek deep into the forest, braving the torrential rain, falling trees and biting ants!

Forest adventure

Setting up a system of camera traps involves a seven-day jungle trek. I go with a team of other workers, including a local tracker who's good at spotting pygmy hippo trails. To decide where to put each camera, I carry a **GPS (Global Positioning System)**. The trackers also have an in-depth knowledge of the forest, and make sure we don't get lost.

A GPS (Global Positioning System) uses signals from satellites to tell us exactly where we are.

Ben and the rest of the team at work setting up a camera trap.

In the forest

The rainforest in Liberia is so dense and remote, we sometimes have to travel up rivers in canoes to get where we want to go. Deep in the jungle, you can hear the calls of colobus monkeys, and I've also spotted spot-nosed monkeys, chimpanzees and snakes. There are lots of creepy-crawlies too.

The forest is thick, hot and very humid, so the air feels really damp. As the day goes on, you get swelteringly hot and sticky. Then, every afternoon, you get soaked to the skin by a rainstorm!

Survival skills

On a trek, we have to drink a lot of water as we sweat so much. It's hard work tramping through the forest, so for food we take beans and rice – they have plenty of energy and protein to keep us going.

At night, it's much too hot for a tent! Instead, we sleep on mats underneath a **tarpaulin** stretched over branches. It can be scary going to sleep, as the wind picks up and sometimes blows a tree over. I never know if I might be underneath one when it falls!

BEN'S TREKKING GEAR CHECKLIST

Large rucksack for carrying everything
Camera traps
GPS, torch and binoculars
Spare batteries
Notebook to write down where I put the cameras
Machete (a large knife) to cut a path through the forest
Camping gear
Food supplies
Water bottle
Iodine tablets to purify drinking water from the streams

Home for the night for Ben and his team.

A pangolin is a strange, long-tailed creature covered in large scales.

CLOSE ENCOUNTER

Meeting a pygmy hippo close up is pretty unlikely – but I did once find a rare giant pangolin (also known as a scaly anteater). I tried to get even closer, but it ran away!

PANGOLIN

SAPO NATIONAL PARK

Sapo National Park in Liberia is an area of natural tropical rainforest – one of the wildest, greenest, and lushest on Earth. It is one of the few places that pygmy hippos live, as well as other wildlife such as elephants, monkeys and chimpanzees, antelopes, snakes, parrots, crocodiles, wild cats and all kinds of creepy-crawlies.

United Nations soldiers had to help clear people out of Sapo National Park after Liberia's civil wars.

A safe home for wildlife

Sapo was first created as a National Park in 1983. To protect the wildlife, there were laws banning anyone from hunting, farming, mining, building, cutting down trees, or living there. More than 30 people had jobs running the park and guarding the wildlife.

Disaster strikes

But when Liberia suffered through its two deadly civil wars, many of the rules were broken. Rebel fighters took over the land and and killed some of the staff, while others escaped. Groups of soldiers and villagers used the park as a hideout, surviving by hunting the wild animals, including the endangered pygmy hippos.

Sapo National Park was badly damaged during Liberia's two civil wars. But the park is now being made a safe place for wildlife again.

SAPO NATIONAL PARK
FULLY PROTECTED BY LAW
ABSOLUTELY NO:
HUNTING, FISHING, FARMING, MINING, LOGGING
AND SETTLEMENT
SCIENTIFIC RESEARCH PERMITTED ONLY BY THE FDA

Gold rush

After civil war ended in 2003, things got even worse. Thousands of people moved into the park, and tried to make a living by logging, looking for gold, or hunting for bushmeat, despite the bans. The Liberian government had to move them, with help from soldiers – but it's very hard to keep everyone out.

Bigger and better

From 2003, the park has started to recover, which is good news for the pygmy hippo. As well as making it bigger, Liberia has made it more secure, and most people who live around it respect the rules. Some local people work as guides. They lead tourists, scientists and other visitors through the forest, and show them how to spot wildlife.

A visitor to Sapo National park makes his way across a stream, led by a guide.

Rare wild chimpanzees can be found in Sapo National Park.

CAN I GO THERE?

Sapo is hard to travel to, and does not yet have facilities for lots of tourists – though that could happen in the future. But people can go there and camp in the park, if they arrange it first with the Liberian Forestry Development Authority in Monrovia. Visitors pay a small fee, and are only allowed to travel in the forest with a proper local guide.

ONE PYGMY HIPPO'S STORY: SNAPPING BORIS

We know very little about how pygmy hippos live in the wild. So the idea of using camera traps to search for them in Sapo National Park was very exciting for conservation workers, and for hippo scientists. Would the cameras finally bring them face-to-face with a wild pygmy hippo?

It took a huge team of people to set up all the cameras in the forest.

How the cameras work

The camera traps used in Sapo are triggered by both heat and motion sensors. When an animal brushes past the camera trap, or walks up to it, it triggers the sensors and the camera takes a picture. As the cameras sense heat rather than light, they can capture a good image of a wild animal, even in the dark. Each camera can take and store 3,000 pictures.

A grid of cameras

Conservation workers position the camera traps in a grid pattern in the forest. There are 32 cameras in each grid, with 2km gaps between them. If two or more different cameras snap the same hippo, the scientists can then can work how and when the hippo moved from one trap to another.

NAMING THE ANIMALS

Conservation workers often give the wild animals they work with their own, human-style names. It helps tell which animal is which quickly and easily, instead of using numbers that are hard to remember. It's especially useful for studying animals that live together in groups, like gorillas or common hippos.

ZSL scientist Dr Ben Collen and a colleague test one of the camera traps by pretending to be pygmy hippos.

"We knew we'd get something or other, but I never dared hope that we'd get pygmy hippos so soon."

ZSL team leader Ben Collen.

Hello Boris!

Just three days after setting up the first camera traps, the team checked for results and saw... a pygmy hippo! Since then, several different hippos have been caught on camera. In this photo, you can see a hippo that the conservation workers in Sapo named Boris. This hippo has a scar on its head that makes him easy to identify.

Boris looks slightly sheepish to be snapped as he wanders past a camera trap – but the ZSL team were delighted to see him!

CONSERVATION BREEDING

Conservation breeding **means helping animals to breed, or have babies, in** captivity **– places like zoos or wildlife parks. This can be a great way to help endangered species. It keeps up the numbers of animals and keeps them healthy and safe.**

Hippos in pairs

Luckily, pygmy hippos and common hippos both breed well in captivity. To help them have calves, zoos around the world move hippos from one place to another, and put them together in pairs, one male and one female. Sometimes, they like each other, mate and have babies – but sometimes they don't.

GOING WILD

Zoos breed some types of endangered species in captivity, then release or **reintroduce** them back into the wild. If it works, it can help to save a species from dying out. It hasn't been tried with pygmy hippos, but it could be one day – when their wild habitat is safe enough to release them into.

This is a very young common hippo who has just started feeding on leaves and plants.

Book of babies

All good zoos that keep hippos work together to make a record called a **studbook**. It makes lists of all the hippos that are in captivity, and all the new hippos that are born. One zoo looks after the studbook for each species. The pygmy hippo studbook is at Zoo Basel, in Basel, Switzerland.

Having a baby

When a mother hippo is pregnant, the zookeepers have to look after her extra-carefully. Like a human mum, a common or pygmy hippo can have an **ultrasound scan** to check that the baby is growing properly. She may also need extra food and vitamins. When it's time for the calf to be born, the mother needs peace and quiet, and is kept away from visitors.

Zoo babies like Sapo could one day be reintroduced into the wild when their habitat is once again safe enough.

BOYS AND GIRLS

Although lots of pygmy hippos have had babies in captivity, there's one small problem – they have more girls than boys. For every two male babies born, there are at least three female ones. This makes it harder to put as many hippos into pairs. Scientists are not sure why it happens.

In the USA, there is an ongoing project to reintroduce the critically endangered red wolf back into the wild.

WHAT NEXT?

It takes a lot of work to turn things around for a vulnerable or endangered species. For those who want to help the endangered pygmy hippo, there's still a long way to go, and plenty to do...

Finding out more

Learning more about pygmy hippos is vital. In many ways, they are still mysterious. Scientists need to find out exactly how many there are, where they are, and what they need most.

A home in the wild

The most urgent thing all hippos need is a safe place to live in the wild. To help save any species, we have to save its natural habitat, and its **ecosystem** – the other plants and animals that live together with it.

National parks such as Sapo can do this for endangered pygmy hippos, but only if they are properly protected and patrolled. So conservation experts are helping Liberia to keep improving Sapo National Park. It is also important to protect habitats across Africa for common hippos, so they do not become endangered like their pygmy hippo cousins.

Common hippos need space and protection so that they can breed and keep up their numbers.

More methods

Other conservation methods, plans and ideas include:

- Helping people in West Africa to learn more about their endangered species and national parks, through things like TV programmes and school lessons.
- Teaching people who live near the hippos how to avoid harming them.
- Helping people to train as wildlife guides, wardens and rangers, so they can get jobs working in national parks, instead of having to hunt.
- Developing **ecotourism** to make it easier for tourists to visit national parks and see the wildlife. Their money then helps to run the parks.
- Using zoos, the Internet, and books like this one to let everyone know about protecting vulnerable and endangered species such as common and pygmy hippos.

GONE FOREVER

In prehistoric times, giant hippos, even bigger than the biggest common hippos today, roamed Europe. More recently, other species of hippos lived on the African island of Madagascar, but became extinct. And a type of pygmy hippo also lived in Nigeria, but disappeared in the last 100 years. The common and pygmy hippos we have today are the last survivors.

The giant panda is an endangered species, but conservation efforts are working well and its numbers are on the rise.

Conservation work happening now is the only thing that can keep the pymgy hippo from extinction.

CAN WE SAVE THE HIPPOS?

What will the future bring for hippos? We don't know yet! But at least we've made a start. Today we try to save vulnerable and endangered species, unlike in the past, when many creatures were wiped out without a second thought.

Are there enough hippos left?

For a species to survive in the wild, there have to be a certain number of them. If there are too few, it becomes too hard for the animals to meet, mate and breed. Then, their numbers fall until they are all gone.

There are still quite a lot of common hippos in the wild. But we have to be careful that their habitats are protected so they do not become endangered.

There are now only 2,000 to 3,000 pygmy hippos left in the wild, and small groups of pygmy hippos are cut off from each other because of habitat loss. This makes it even harder for them to meet and breed.

The Amur leopard is a species that has become so rare, it's very difficult for it to breed successfully.

MONEY MATTERS

Conservation work, such as scientific study, running national parks and zoos, conservation breeding, and education, costs a lot of money. ZSL and other organisations need a constant supply of money to carry on their work.

Adoptions

Thug the pygmy hippo

Adopt Thug, ZSL London Zoo's pygmy hippo.

The perfect Christmas gift for any gentle giants.

Contrary to his name, Thug is a gentle soul who loves to swim and sleep. However he does enjoy chasing companion Nicky-noo around.

Just like most couples, they occasionally squabble over who gets what place in the heated shelter.

By adopting Thug for yourself or as a gift, you will be directly supporting ZSL's conservation work.

are posted out in an attractive presentation folder which contains: a letter with fun facts about your animal, personalised certificate, zoo ticket, Wild About magazine and a photograph of your

via a welcome email includes; a free e-ticket to the zoo, access to animal web pages, a personalised e-certificate, subscription to magazine and e-mail updates.

Visit the adoption centre

Adopting endangered species is a fun and easy way to help them.

These tourists are going on a forest trek in Thailand to watch wildlife.

Thinking about the future

People hunt endangered species and cut down forests because they desperately need food or money. But it doesn't make sense in the long term. Once a forest ecosystem is gone, or a species dies out, it can never come back.

By protecting habitats and species, people can make a living from ecotourism. This is happening in more and more places around the world, and it is helping many endangered species.

HOW CAN YOU HELP?

- Adopt a hippo. You (or your family or class) can sponsor a hippo in a zoo or in a conservation area, and get updates about how it's doing.
- Visit a zoo – the fee helps the zoo to look after, breed and study endangered animals.
- Be an ecotourist – on holiday, pay to see amazing wildlife in a national park or reserve.
- Never buy products made from endangered species.
- Do it yourself! Study science subjects, biology, zoology or **animal husbandry**, and you could become a zookeeper, vet, scientist or ranger working with endangered species.

ABOUT ZSL

The Zoological Society of London (ZSL) is a charity that provides conservation support for animals both in the UK and worldwide. We also run ZSL London Zoo and ZSL Whipsnade Zoo.

Our work in the wild extends to Africa, where our conservationists and scientists are working to protect pygmy hippos from extinction. These amazing mammals are part of ZSL's EDGE of Existence programme, which is specially designed to focus on genetically distinct animals that are struggling for survival.

By buying this book, you have helped us raise money to continue our conservation work with hippos and other animals in need of protection. Thank you.

To find out more about ZSL and how you can become further involved with our work visit **zsl.org** and **zsl.org/edge**

Pygmy hippos are amazing animals, and with conservation and education we can help them to survive.

Websites
Pygmy Hippo at EDGE of Existence
www.zsl.org/edge
Pygmy Hippo at ZSL London Zoo
www.zsl.org/pygmyhippo
Adopt a Pygmy Hippo
www.zsl.org/adoptpygmyhippo
Common Hippo at ZSL Whipsnade Zoo
www.zsl.org/commonhippo

Places to visit
ZSL London Zoo
Outer Circle, Regent's Park, London,
NW1 4RY, UK
www.zsl.org/london
0844 225 1826

ZSL Whipsnade Zoo
Dunstable, Bedfordshire, LU6 2LF, UK
www.zsl.org/whipsnade
0844 225 1826

To survive in the wild, hippos need the right natural habitats, with water, space and food plants.

It's important to help hippos to breed, as this is how they can recover their numbers.

GLOSSARY

adapt Change over time to suit the surroundings.

aggressive Easily annoyed or violent.

animal husbandry Looking after and breeding animals.

bacteria A type of tiny living thing.

bloat A name for a group of hippos.

blood diamonds Diamonds sold to raise money for fighting a war.

blood sweat Reddish substance released from a hippo's skin.

breed Mate and have babies.

bull A male hippo.

bushmeat Meat that comes from wild animals.

calf A baby hippo.

captivity Being kept in a zoo, wildlife park or garden.

civil war A war between different sides within the same country.

conservation Protecting nature and wildlife.

conservation breeding Breeding animals in zoos.

cow A female hippo.

digestive system Organs that take in food and pass it through the body.

dominant In charge or in the top position.

ecosystem A habitat and the living things that are found in it.

ecotourism Visiting wild places as a tourist to see wildlife.

EDGE Short for Evolutionarily Distinct and Globally Endangered.

election People of a country choosing who they want to be their leaders.

enclosure A secure pen, cage or other home or for a zoo animal.

endangered At risk of dying out and become extinct.

extinct No longer existing.

government The group of people in charge of country.

GPS Short for Global Positioning System, a way of finding where you are.

graze To nibble constantly at food.

habitat The natural surroundings that a species lives in.

habitat fragmentation Breaking up natural habitat into small areas.

habitat loss Damaging or destroying habitat.

herbivore pellets Special food for pet or zoo herbivores, or plant-eaters.

infra-red camera A camera that detects infra-red light or heat.

intestines Tubes that carry food through the body.

IUCN Short for the International Union for Conservation of Nature

lice Small insects that live on other animals.

logging Cutting down trees.

mammal A kind of animal that feeds its babies on milk from its body.

monitor To check, measure or keep track of something.

national park A protected area of land where wildlife can live safely.

poaching Hunting animals that are protected by law and shouldn't be hunted.

pod A name for a group of hippos.

range The area where a species lives.

rebels People who fight against their leaders.

reintroduce To release a species back into the wild.

shoot The first growth of a plant from a seed.

species A particular type of living thing.

studbook A record of the animals of a particular species born in captivity.

tarpaulin A sheet of material made of plastic or waterproof canvas.

territory An area that an animal considers its own.

tsunami A series of powerful waves caused by sea water being disturbed.

ultrasound scan A way of using sound waves to look inside the body.

vulnerable At risk, but not as seriously as an endangered species.

wildlife reserve A protected area of land where wildlife can live safely.

ZSL Short for Zoological Society of London.

FIND OUT MORE

Books

Helping Hippos by Jill Eggleton, Scholastic, 2011

Owen and Mzee: A Little Story about Big Love by Michelle Y. Glennon, GDG Publishing, 2007

Nature Watch: Hippos by Sally M. Walker, Lerner Publications, 2008

What's it Like to be a... Zoo Keeper? by Elizabeth Dowen and Lisa Thompson, A&C Black 2010

Websites

San Diego Zoo: Pygmy Hippopotamus
www.sandiegozoo.org/animalbytes/t-pygmy_hippo.html

Pygmy Hippo Webcam
www.marwell.org.uk/interactive_zone/webcams.asp

Fauna and Flora International
www.fauna-flora.org/species/pygmy-hippo

Places to visit

Bristol Zoo Gardens
Clifton, Bristol, BS8 3HA, UK
www.bristolzoo.org.uk/
0117 974 7399

Edinburgh Zoo
Corstorphine, Edinburgh,
Scotland, EH12 6TS
www.edinburghzoo.org.uk/
0131 334 9171

Zoo Basel
Binningerstrasse 40, Basel,
Switzerland
www.zoobasel.ch/e

San Diego Zoo
2920 Zoo Drive, Balboa Park,
San Diego, California, USA
www.sandiegozoo.org

Brookfield Zoo
8400 31st Street, Brookfield,
IL 60513, Chicago, USA
www.brookfieldzoo.org

INDEX

OTHER TITLES IN THE ANIMALS ON THE EDGE SERIES

www.storiesfromthezoo.com

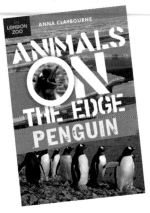

Penguin
ISBN: HB 978-1-4081-4822-8
PB 978-1-4081-4960-7

Rhino
ISBN: HB 978-1-4081-4823-5
PB 978-1-4081-4956-0

Tiger
ISBN: HB 978-1-4081-4824-2
PB 978-1-4081-4957-7

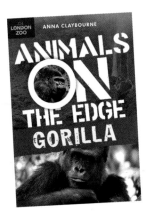

Gorilla
ISBN: HB 978-1-4081-4825-9
PB 978-1-4081-4959-1

Elephant
ISBN: HB 978-1-4081-4827-3
PB 978-1-4081-4958-4